THE
RAINFOREST
QUEEN

A NOVEL

CLIFF RATZA

THE RAINFOREST QUEEN

A NOVEL

CLIFF RATZA

The Rainforest Queen is the first novelette in our alternate history series, "The Rainforest Chronicles." Yarima, the leader of an all-female Yanomami rainforest tribe, has just begun to see the dangers posed by the European explorers from the East, who call themselves conquistadors, to her land, people, and way of life. She has heard from tribes to the west that an explorer from a land across the western ocean might have what she needs to defeat this threat, so she travels to meet him at a tribal village on that ocean's shore.

There, she meets Tianshu, who comes from China. He is on a mission to explore the South American continent, learning about the land, its tribes, and the riches it might offer in exchange for his help, and to assess the damage that European colonization leaves in its wake. He and Yarima plan an expedition that will accomplish his goals and hers.

So, follow the action starting on page one and leading to a thrilling conclusion on the very last page as they join forces to battle the conquistadors.

The theme of this novelette is particularly relevant today. Indigenous people anywhere deserve the respect and support from all nations. Most anthropologists now credit them with a greater understanding of their world and having a sophisticated culture worth fighting to preserve.

So, thank you for joining the adventure.

Dedication

I am eternally grateful to my parents, Clyde and Betty Ratza, for all they gave and did for me. Mother was a reader par excellence, and I believe she would have enjoyed reading my books to Father, so I always begin dedications by mentioning this "Royal Pair."

And I thank my sister, Claudia, for showing me the beauty of prose and poetry. Thanks to Sandra Cruz for her beta reading skill, to Robert Williams and the Production Department at the Quippy Quill, and to John Kane at the Lightning Brain Press for their book marketing expertise.

I dedicate this novelette to the readers of alternate history who want an exciting adventure that goes from the first page to the very last, presenting one such possibility for South America.

Contents

Chapter 1

"Marvels of the Rainforest Sky"

The rainforest sky determined Yarima's favorite times that occurred every day: the radiant orb heralding brightness as it rose, and the fading light signaling darkness as it closed in. The Warrior Queen observed these special events in a manner befitting her position as the leader of an all-female Yanomami rainforest tribe—two of her strongest warriors would paddle her and her daughter, Princess Borea, past their thatched huts along the shores of the mighty Amaru Mayu, the so-called "Mother Serpent of the World."

The tribal priestess and healer had taught Yarima all this, as well as their counting, calendar, and spoken language, along with pictorial writing to record tribal history. Yarima estimated she had lived long enough for six handfuls of fingers, and her daughter for two.

Yarima filled the other times of every day by directing a tribal council, which kept the tribe among the most powerful in their part of the forest, bordered by tributaries and other tribes. She had been even more successful than her warrior queen mother and wanted Borea to carry on when she could no longer lead.

Sometimes, when rays of brightness streamed through the rainforest, Yarima used her powerful yet lithe body to climb with the speed of a jaguar to the top of a tree simply for the joy of viewing an endless sea of green stretching to the horizon whichever way she looked. And at other times, when the unmistakable fragrance coming from the trees, accompanied by a misty veil rising from the rainforest floor and obscuring the footpaths, or when refreshing water poured from the sky through protective leaves of the trees, she would dance for the joy of being alive.

But even with help from her tribal council, concerns and problems filled most of her time every day. The invaders from across the waters to the East—the so-called European Explorers, who called themselves Portuguese conquistadors—posed her current challenge. Soon, she would lead a meeting with them to limit their exploitation, and she would bring her priestess and healer to translate their strange tongue. In the future, she wanted to know enough about their customs, ways, and words to understand for herself, no longer needing an interpreter.

Chapter 2

"The Invader's Village"

Pedro Álvares Cabral and his conquistadors from Portugal needed to exercise caution when encountering tribes while traveling inland along the Amazon River, especially when confronting the black-haired, tall, and ferocious women warriors. Although equipped with swords and muskets, his bulky men were no match for the speed and spears of the women when clashing in the rainforest.

Depending on where the confrontation occurred, the women would sometimes leap from tree limbs onto his men. Then, other warriors would unerringly jab them with spears, even if they were wearing helmets and body armor. The oppressive heat and moisture dripping from the air wore his men out, but the warriors never seemed to tire.

Today, he would use gifts to barter for safe passage as he and his men explored further upriver. This would be his second meeting with Queen Yarima. She and her warriors would emerge from the rainforest bordering his encampment on the riverbank faster than his men could prepare, which meant only Pedro and two trusted guards would meet with Yarima, her priestess, and her healer.

When one of his men yelled,

"They're here," Pedro and his guards marched to meet them. Pedro spoke first after bowing to show respect.

"Oh, powerful Queen, we are pleased you have come."

Yarima's nod showed she understood, but let her priestess reply.

"We know what you want, but what will you give us in return?"

"I have gifts of coconuts, fabric, bracelets, and necklaces if you will let us go further upriver. Let me show them to you." His guards ran to get them and soon returned with them.

All three women wore pleased smiles when examining them, and after conferring in a language Pedro did not understand, the priestess said,

"You have safe passage as far as our tribal land goes. We will watch you, and every time you see us, you must have more of these gifts to give us."

"Thank you, powerful Queen. We will have them ready."

After Yarima gave a farewell gesture, she and her people melted into the rainforest, leaving Pedro and his guards stunned by their stealth.

Yarima's tribe gathered around her as soon as she returned, waiting for her to speak, which she did as soon as she placed the items in front.

"We have brought back gifts for the invaders' safe passage. Come, take what you want. They will give us more when we see them paddling upriver." As her warriors examined them, Yarima and her council of wise elders convened in their circular longhouse.

Yarima felt that she now knew enough to speak for herself.

"These conquistadors have weapons that spit fire and magic that lights up the night. There are also stories that they ride gigantic beasts that trample everyone in their way. They won't share any of this, and we must have some if our way of life is to survive. Our priestess and healer will help me find a path forward, and while we are doing that, have everyone return to their tribal duties. Make sure one of the elder women teaches Borea the customs of our tribe and the ways of the rainforest. When time permits, I might listen…"

Yarima spent most of the days that followed looking for a path forward, but one day she paused to listen to an elder teaching Borea about animals.

"Rainforest creatures can be deadly. Stay far away from jaguars and anacondas. They can sneak through the forest and swim in the river. If an anaconda catches you, it will coil around and squeeze your life out before swallowing you whole."

Borea shuddered but said nothing, so the elder continued.

"And when on the river, watch out for big-mouth animals with teeth that can bite off arms and legs."

Borea shook her head but still said nothing, so the elder said more.

"Don't chase after any brightly colored frogs. One touch is enough to kill you. The same goes for the wandering spider. It's as wide as your hand, and its bite is deadly."

Borea finally asked a question.

"Aren't there some animals we can eat?"

"Yes, some types of crawling or flying bugs, and some kinds of fish. You'll learn which are good when we take you bug hunting and spear fishing…"

Many days passed until Yarima found a path forward, which she described at the next council meeting.

"Tribes bordering toward the setting sun have told us about explorers coming from across those waters. They have not yet reached our rainforest, but they are supposed to be better than the invaders we have met. It is time I travel to meet them. Our priestess and healer will pick warriors to come with us. We shall leave soon…"

Chapter 3

"Reaching Out to Explorers from Beyond the Setting Sun"

Yarima found guides along the way who led them through passes and valleys rather than climbing snow-covered mountains. The guides knew who and where to meet the person who could help deal with the conquistadors. Many days later, they arrived.

Emperor Jingtai of the Ming dynasty had selected Tianshu to lead a special voyage because, as a young explorer, he had gained experience and fame while serving under eunuch admiral Zheng on all seven of his massive voyages seeking treasure in far-flung lands. Now much older and wiser, Tianshu had just landed on the western shore of the continent that the Europeans wanted to colonize. His goal: explore firsthand what opportunities awaited his emperor and himself.

Tianshu already knew about European explorers reaching the New World, and he had just begun planning how to reach his goal when messengers told him that a warrior queen from the other side of the mountains wanted to talk with him. Today would be their very first meeting.

Yarima studied the features of the man standing before her, who was about to speak.

He looks different than the conquistadors…less bulky with yellowish skin and a flatter forehead…more shape to his cheeks, and a slant to his eyes…he knows different tongues…I hope he keeps speaking like the Europeans so I can understand and speak for myself.

Yarima hid her relief when he did.

"My name is Tianshu. Messengers say you want to talk with me. Please tell me who you are and where you come from."

"I am Yarima, warrior queen of the Yanomami people from the land on the other side of the mountains. My tribe lives in the rainforest along the banks of the mighty Amazon River. Do your people know of us?"

"We have learned some things from listening to what European explorers say. I am leading a voyage from my land across the sea to explore your continent. The messengers say you need my help. What do you want?"

"I seek your help in protecting my land and tribe from the conquistadors. They have little respect for my rainforest or people, take the treasures buried in the land and its plants, and have weapons and magic more powerful than mine. I have heard that your people are better. I will give you some of our treasures if you will help me fight them using better weapons and better ways of attacking."

Tianshu considered for several moments what he had just heard before replying.

"We are respectful of other people and their lands, and we have weapons like theirs, called muskets and swords. And my wise elders have studied the world. We now know some of the rules that are better than magic. I am willing to help, but I must sail back to my country to load more ships with what you want and then lead a flotilla to the mouth of your Amazon River, where we will anchor while I lead my men along the riverbank until we find you and your tribe."

"How long will it take you to reach my village?"

"It could take half a year."

"Very well. I am leaving now and will await your arrival. You know more than my people. Will you show us how to make fires that will light the night, and tell us more about the world?"

"Yes, and we have other things you might want. The more you know, the better for my people, too."

Yarima bowed to end the meeting. Then, she and her warriors started their homeward journey.

Chapter 4

"Rituals and Celebrations While Waiting"

The tribe gathered around Yarima as soon as she returned so they could hear what she had accomplished.

"I have found people from a land across the water who will help us fight the conquistadors, if we give them some of the treasures in our rainforest. When they arrive, they will also teach us more about the world and bring us weapons and tools. I told their leader how to find our village, but it will take him many months to get here. Until then, everyone must keep doing their tribal duties…"

Yarima filled her days fulfilling hers while enjoying morning canoe trips on the river, but on one trip many days later, the canoe bumped into something that dumped everyone into the water. A wide-jawed animal with rows of teeth had tipped it over, and before her warriors could beat it off with paddles, it seized Borea's leg and started dragging her under. Yarima grabbed both arms while pulling and screaming, but she couldn't free Borea. The last she saw were her eyes wide with fear and her mouth filled with water. The paddlers knew she would soon be dead, so they pulled Yarima away, righted the canoe, and paddled back to the village.

As soon as she reported the catastrophe, the priestess spoke.

"You must give us another princess. You must take part in our next fertility ritual. I will contact a neighboring tribe, so their strongest males know what we want..."

Moonlight gave them what they needed several days later. Yarima danced to tribal chants with her warriors, who, like their queen, felt jolts of passion in special places. Then they chose males who had gathered to complete the ritual. Yarima's pleasure lasted until daylight.

During the following days, Yarima and her warriors watched the conquistadors and became alarmed at their activities, so she led a meeting with the council of wise elders.

"The conquistadors are taking more and giving less. We must assemble a war party for me to lead an attack in our rainforest just before the sun deserts the sky. That's when we will have the most advantage."

The priestess and healer looked at one another before the priestess spoke.

"Some of our warriors may die, but you must survive. The healer and I will choose your war party and pick the time to attack. Make sure you come back..."

Pedro liked everything his conquistadors had achieved. They planted more palm trees bearing coconuts, found additional places upriver for building huts, and continued stripping the land of its wealth. He was about to eat slices of anaconda roasted over a fire when two guards screamed from opposite ends of the encampment.

"The Amazon warriors are attacking. Push them back..."

Stepping backward, Pedro gasped as the females killed many more of his men than vice versa. They leaped with agility and jabbed with spears faster than his men could defend themselves. The battle ended when the females vanished back into the forest.

Yarima's warriors carried their fallen sisters as she led them back to the village. While trekking, Yarima decided what she would do.

Upon returning, she gathered the tribe about her.

"We have halted the conquistadors, at least for now. Our warriors killed many, and we stopped to keep the number of our wounded from growing. It is time for our priestess to conduct a ceremony that honors all our warriors for protecting us, those still alive and those who died in battle. Then, we will bury them in our sacred ground…"

The ceremony began as soon as the priestess directed her acolytes regarding preparation and chants, and it lasted until the first rays of light streamed through the trees.

Several days later, Yarima led another meeting with the council.

"The time of shortest daylight is approaching, so we must plan our celebration marking the return of more daylight. This time, we must mention all the good that has happened and what we expect in the days that will follow. Be sure to say we await the return of Tianshu, whose people will help us fight the conquistadors. And until then, we must do our best to survive and keep our rainforest tribe alive…"

Chapter 5

"The Arrival"

When several warriors rushed to tell Yarima that they had spotted Tianshu, they led her back so she could confirm that he had come. The sun was high overhead, so they had no trouble retracing their steps. When she reached him, she waited for him to speak.

"I have returned, Queen Yarima, and my men are carrying even more than what you need. Lead us to your village, and we shall give them to you."

Yarima didn't need to speak. Her bow said all she had to.

Her council of wise elders had prepared a place for Tianshu and his men to stay by the time they reached the village. After they piled the gifts in an open area, the priestess led a chant before everyone ate. Afterward, Yarima took him to the council's longhouse, where they were waiting for him to speak.

"I will leave two of my wisest men when I leave, because there is much you must know about the world. My people have learned much from others, and we will teach you more about the Europeans and their language, but I will start by showing you what the world looks like. Please have someone give me a coconut."

Soon, he was scratching its surface to match what he was saying.

"The world is round, like this coconut, and it is solid all the way through. You might think our land is flat, but it isn't. We live on the surface, which is divided into land masses called continents that are separated by vast expanses of water called oceans. We call the world Earth, and it spins on a line connecting two points called poles, one at the top, and the other at the bottom."

Tianshu paused to point. When Yarma said,

"I see," he said more while pointing.

"The continents have names. Here is Europe, and here is Asia. That is where my people live, in a country called China. Here is Africa, and here is a place called North America, the so-called New World. And below it is your continent, which is called South America."

Yarima said,

"We are on opposite sides of the world. How do you keep from getting lost?"

"My wisest people invented long, long ago a pointing device called a compass. One end points to the North Pole, which is at the top. The other points to the South Pole, which is at the bottom. Let me give the coconut to you right now, and you can explain to your council members what you have just learned."

After doing so with no coaching, Tianshu said,

"You are smart. No wonder you are the queen. Why don't we rest until tomorrow? Then, my wise men will begin teaching more."

Tianshu spent the rest of the day talking with Yarima while following her. Before joining his men as darkness descended, he made a personal observation.

"You look like you are bearing a child. Has your healer said the same?"

"Yes, and I hope you will teach us about your calendar, so my tribe will know how to keep better track of time."

"My wise men will do that, but not even they or our healers know if the infant will be male or female. What does your tribe do if it is a boy?"

"Some female tribes kill them, but we exchange the boy for a girl. That way, everyone is better off."

"Indeed. Well, rest now, so you will be ready to learn more tomorrow…"

In the days that followed, the wise men emphasized topics that, according to Tianshu, would be useful for everyone. They started by explaining how to use the calendar that divides the year into months, weeks, and days, how to tell time that divides a day into hours, and how the European culture differs from China's. Then, they showed how to start a fire and use the weapons they brought.

Later, they covered topics of more interest to the priestess or healer, and in all cases, Tianshu served as Yarima's personal teacher. He followed her whenever she left the teaching session to deal with more pressing matters.

After several weeks, Tianshu knew he must leave.

My wise men will stay and teach more, but Yarima is smart enough to figure things out on her own, and I will teach her more when she needs it.

When he told her this, she knew what to say.

"I thought so. You must do more exploring. Where will you go next?"

Tianshu replied with a question of his own.

"Have you traveled beyond the borders of your rainforest?"

"No, there has been no need. Why do you ask?"

"I need to visit other native tribes that inhabit other places in South America to assess the damage European colonization has left behind."

Yarima's puzzled look came with her words.

"What is European colonization?"

"The Europeans want to kill the natives using the weapons and diseases they bring, take the land, and have their people move in. That's not what China wants. I am here to learn about the land and its native tribes, and then work with them as a partner to help one another. We are more thoughtful and respectful than the Europeans. We will give them tools and medicine to help fight the conquistadors. And to do this, I need your help."

"What can I do?"

"Bring a group of your warriors and explore with me. I have heard that you strike fear into conquistadors, so they might not try to attack us. Other tribes don't defend themselves as well as yours. Bring a group of warriors, and together we will fight the conquistadors."

"I will do so as soon as I give birth."

Tianshu nodded, then said,

"And you can translate languages when we come across new tribes. Your tongue is better than mine for doing so."

"Where shall we meet?"

"I am building a more permanent encampment on the banks of the Amazon where it meets the Atlantic Ocean. When you arrive, I shall train your warriors in better ways of fighting. I call them strategies, and centuries ago, China's military leader, Sun Tsu, wrote a book called 'On Warfare.' Together, you and I shall be formidable."

"My healer says I will give birth in two months. Soon after, we will meet again…"

Chapter 6

"Meeting New Tribes"

Concocted from tree bark and plants, the salve and potion Yarima's healer gave helped speed her recovery after giving birth to a female. Three weeks later, she told the priestess to choose another nursing mother to care for Mandei while she was away, and a week later, she picked twenty of her warriors whom she would lead to join Tianshu. The priestess led a chant that heralded their departure.

The early morning sunlight filtering through the trees along the riverbank filled Yarima with joy as it sparkled off the water.

I have lived my entire life in this beautiful rainforest, but now I know enough to feel excited, not fearful, about exploring new lands and meeting new tribes. I will bring back more gifts and knowledge for my tribe.

Mid-morning two days later, when Yarima came upon Tianshu's garrison, his spotters must have seen them, because he was waiting to greet her and spoke first.

"You and your warriors look ready, and you brought the right number for our first expedition. Please settle into a couple of the empty huts and then come to the longhouse for training to begin after having something to eat."

A short time later, Tianshu spoke to the group.

"I have brought back weapons that are better than what you have—metal-tipped spears and muskets. You already know how to use the spears, but we will teach you how to use muskets. They need gunpowder, and we will also teach you to make fire.

"But I will start by teaching you what Sun Tsu, our leading military general and battle planner, taught long ago. My country has saved this knowledge in a book called 'The Art of War.' I will review its teachings, and afterward, Yarima will tell us what she learned."

After Yarima nodded, he continued.

"Sun Tzu's 'The Art of War' teaches that conducting a battle involves extensive prior planning, understanding of both your own and the enemy's strengths and weaknesses, and a commitment to achieving victory with minimal fighting through strategic maneuver and tactics. Key principles include knowing when to fight and when not to, the importance of terrain and weather, leadership and discipline, and flexibility and deception to confuse the enemy and secure an advantageous position. The ultimate goal is to subdue the enemy without engaging in battle, making victory complete, and preserving resources."

Tianshu covered the material again, answering all questions that came up, and after a mid-afternoon break, he asked Yarima to summarize.

She stood while speaking.

"We must know ourselves and our enemy, because victory depends on understanding our and the enemy's strengths and weaknesses. That is why planning is so important. If do it well enough, we might win without fighting.

"And to do that, we must be deceptive by appearing weak when strong and vice versa, controlling the battle, adapting to what's happening, and paying attention to the terrain and the weather. As your leader, I must make sure my warriors have the training and discipline needed, which will minimize our wounded and the use of our resources."

After she sat, Tianshu said,

"In the coming days, we will go over this again while practicing tactics with the weapons I have brought…"

During the two weeks that followed, Yarima and her warriors perfected their battle preparation and fighting skills. Yarima now knew how to organize her warriors by dividing them into groups that would focus on different conquistador positions before massing for the final attack.

When Tianshu sensed they were ready, he took Yarima aside.

"Tomorrow, we start exploring new territory. My tracker has already found trails leading inland to the north. He will lead with the two of us right behind. My men will follow and carry our supplies, while your warriors space themselves from front to back, ready to protect us from any attacks."

"How far will we go?"

"Until we must turn back for more supplies. But we replenish food and water from the land and tribes we meet."

"I hope to find new plants and seeds that I can bring back to my food gatherers and learn the ways of the tribes we meet."

"All that and more is possible. We shall see as we go…"

Yarima marveled to herself as the expedition started.

How beautiful—the land has rolling hills carpeted in lush green grasses and forests of trees different than those in my rainforest. The weather stays pleasant, but it feels cooler the further we go. Although we haven't met a tribe yet, I think they could survive on this kind of land…

Three days later, they came across a partially destroyed village and its tribe, whose chieftain warily confronted them, speaking in a tongue Yarima could understand.

"I am Yarima of the Yanomami rainforest tribe. With me is Tianshu, an explorer who comes from a land called China that is across the ocean to the west. We come to learn about your tribe and customs, and we might have items that will help. We are different from the conquistadors, who came from the east. Do you know them?"

"Yes, they killed some of my people and destroyed some of my village. They are more powerful than the network of tribes we belong to. They left a disease that killed more, and when they return, we won't be able to drive them away."

After interpreting, Tianshu told her what to say, which she did while pointing.

"He has the weapons and skills to defeat them. Please let us demonstrate…"

After doing so, the chieftain said,

"I will gather leaders and fighters from other tribes, so they can see what you offer. Helping all of us will help you even more."

Tianshu and Yarima trained them in the two weeks that followed, and in a quiet moment, he thought to himself what he was seeing.

These tribes are much more than merely hunter-gatherers. They have a self-sufficient civilization with a system of religion, government, and their knowledge of the past helps them survive. They will be better off if European colonization leaves them alone…

A day later, Tianshu spoke privately to Yarima.

"They have learned enough to join us on a hunt for the conquistadors. Let's call a meeting for me to explain what we shall do…"

Later that day, Yarima translated for him.

"You have shown the ability to use new weapons. It is time for you to join us and begin fighting the conquistadors. Your trackers will lead us while some of you carry supplies, and when we find them, Yarima and her warriors will group your fighters and tell them what to do. We will leave tomorrow at first light…"

After everyone dispersed, Tianshu spoke further to Yarima.

"These people know some may die in battle, but their religion tells them that their spirit will live on. Does your priestess say the same?"

"Yes, and it helps my warriors when going into battle. I don't believe it; I've never seen or sensed spirits living in the rainforest, but I tell my warriors I do."

"That is wise. Always agree with your priestess to keep your tribe motivated…"

The expedition hiked to the north and east along the trail last taken by the conquistadors. At the end of the second day, when the tracker rushed to tell that he had spotted the conquistadors, Tianshu gathered everyone, and Yarima translated.

"We attack tomorrow. Now rest, and be ready for victory at dawn…

Chapter 7

"The Battle Begins"

The warriors' charge caught Pedro's guards by surprise, because they were having the first meal of the day with all the other conquistadors. When finally spotting the attack, they picked up their weapons and yelled,

"Push them back," before the chaotic battle began.

Dividing into groups led by women warriors, the attackers used weapons like the conquistadors and had a battle strategy the conquistadors had never seen before. Female warriors would pounce on a conquistador, and another attacker would jab with a spear or sword with a speed and fury unmatched. After gaping at the warriors slaying too many of his men, Pedro screamed,

"Retreat, follow me."

They raced away, and when Pedro saw the attackers had stopped chasing, he slowed to a walk, his grinding his teeth and glowering expression matching his thoughts.

I spotted Yarima leading the attack. Where did she get the weapons? How did she learn to fight like that? I need to find other weapons that will give me the advantage...

Gathering around Tianshu, everyone waited for him to speak.

"Our fighters performed well, and we have defeated the invaders. Let us prepare to return to our villages..."

Tianshu saw that some tribes buried the dead where they had fallen, while others arranged to carry them back. He noticed that Yarima's warriors buried theirs, but he didn't ask why.

The return took less time because the victory had energized the group. All the fighters departed for their villages when reaching the starting point, leaving Tianshu and his men along with Yarima and her warriors to talk with the chieftain.

Tianshu said,

"We will continue looking for more tribes tomorrow after resting and restocking with food and water. Will your tracker point us to the path that will lead us to them?"

"Yes, and I hope you will bring us more weapons and medicine when you return. Now that you have trained us, we need them to continue fighting."

"I shall, but I must I must return to my country to replenish the supply, and it might take a year. Until then, have your tribal network band together…"

Tianshu's expedition trekked northward at first light, with one of Tianshu's trackers in the lead. The terrain remained the same, and Yarima spotted no new plants. They hiked for several days, coming across tribes that had similar stories regarding the conquistadors. When Yarima explained why they had come, they were happy that she and Tianshu would train them to fight.

A day later, they met another tribe that had only heard about the conquistadors but would like to be trained. When they gave the expedition food and something to drink, Tianshu knew what he was drinking.

"In my country, we call this tea. We brew it from the leaves of the plant."

When hearing this, Yarima said, "Would you give me some plants and herbs I can take back to my village?"

The tribal leader said,

"Yes, and return someday to train us with your weapons…"

After hiking further for several days, Tianshu told his explorers they must head back.

"We have traveled for too many days, and the end of the continent is nowhere in sight…"

When they reached the garrison nearly a month later, Tianshu gathered the entire expedition.

"I must sail home to tell my emperor what I have learned and then return with more of what the tribes need. You and your warriors should rest and then return to your rainforest."

Yarima's smile accompanied her words.

"Our tribe will want to hear our stories, and our gatherers will want to plant what we have brought back. Will it take an entire year for you to return?"

"I do not know, but until I do, go about your daily lives. And when I do, I will come to your village and look for you…"

Chapter 8
May 2237

"A Return to the Normal World"

Yarima gathered everyone in her village as soon as she and her warriors returned. After she told them about what she had learned and brought back, she paused to hear what the priestess and healer had to say. The priestess spoke first.

"You must visit the other villages in our rainforest network. They might want the weapons and compass you now have and your new methods of fighting and lighting fires."

"I had already thought of that, and I will give the tea plants to our gatherers, so they can make tea. I think everyone will enjoy its taste."

The healer spoke next.

"And I will plant the herbs to make medicines."

"Good. Tianshu will return in a year, so I can do more exploring with him. And until then, we should continue with our normal duties…"

After the meeting, Yarima looked for the nursing mother who had been taking care of her daughter. The mother gave her Mandei, whose cooing showed she instinctively recognized her birth mother.

"I enjoyed taking care of her. She is healthy and easy to care for. Have you returned permanently?"

"Only for the next year. Will you take care of her when I continue exploring?"

"Yes, she and my daughter will become playmates and learn together..."

Yarima assembled a group of warriors the next day and started visiting other villages. Several days later, after getting the reactions the priestess had predicted, she returned.

After reporting the results to the priestess, Yarima continued.

"I want to visit tribes on the other side of the mountains to the west. I will leave in several days..."

She found the guides who had led her the first time to the village where she first met Tianshu. When the leader greeted her, she explained why she had returned.

"For nearly a year, Tianshu and I explored the land to the east, meeting new tribes and learning more about the conquistadors. After we have something to eat and rest, let me tell you my story tomorrow..."

After doing so, when Yarima asked about the tribes and land in his network, the leader answered.

"Whether to the north or south, the conquistadors have not gone there. These lands are not what the conquistadors are looking for. They are long and narrow, bounded by the ocean on one side and the mountains on the other. They are cold and unsuitable for growing crops, and they also have deserts."

"That's good to know. I will tell this to Tianshu..."

When Tianshu reached China's capital city, Beijing, he spoke to the emperor and a group of his wisest government bureaucrats, telling the story about what his exploration had uncovered.

"South America is a vast continent whose primitive people live in small villages. Though they know little and lack the tools we possess, they are smart. I found one such tribe that reminds me of the Amazons talked about in Greek mythology.

"They are powerful female warriors living in a rainforest I explored by traveling inland on a river they also call the Amazon. Like the other tribes I met, they need our help fighting the European conquistador invaders who want to colonize the continent. They will pay for better weapons and tools with silver and tea. If you allow me to explore further, I will learn more and might discover other things they possess that we could use."

The bureaucrats talked until the emperor ended the discussion. His frown matched his words.

"We have known about the Europeans since the days of Marco Polo. They are unpleasant and backward, and now they want to colonize South America. I authorize you to sail back with a larger fleet, carrying what the tribes need to fight the conquistadors, and to explore more of the continent. Bring silk with you. The women warriors might like it."

Tianshu bowed before saying,

"Thank you. I shall make plans to leave as soon as possible."

Chapter 9

"Exploring North and South"

As soon as Tianshu's fleet anchored at the mouth of the Amazon, he sent a messenger led by his tracker to find Yarima. Two days later, the messenger told her to assemble a group of warriors like the previous expedition and follow them to join Tianshu's new expedition.

Yarima knew this day was coming and had already made her plans, so she summoned the tribe, telling all that she and her hand-picked warriors would leave tomorrow to join forces with Tianshu.

She fought back tears that night when giving Mandei to the surrogate mother, but knew she must explore further for the good of all tribes.

Tianshu welcomed them when they arrived, and after they ate, gave them the silk gift.

"Chinese women enjoy making clothing from this fabric, and I think you will too."

Yarima fingered it for a moment before handing it to another warrior. Everyone looked pleased after touching it and brushing it against their cheeks.

Then, explained his plan for how his men and Yarima's warriors would conduct the expedition.

"I have returned with what the tribes we met last time need, so we will travel north to give them to the chieftain at the first village we encountered last time, and let him distribute the items to the other tribes. Then, we trek south of the river to explore the land and discover what tribes live there. Even my emperor's wisest bureaucrats have no clue about what we might find, but he wants us to proceed. So, rest tonight. Tomorrow we pack what we will take heading north. We will leave at first light the next day..."

Tianshu's tracker led the way with Tianshu and Yarima right behind. Two days later, they reached the chieftain's village, and explained why they had returned. The expedition headed south soon after they gave him what they had brought.

They rested a day after returning to the starting point, then left early the next morning to explore south of the river. While hiking, Tianshu and Yarima conversed occasionally, with Yarima doing most of the talking.

After several days, she mentioned what she had been seeing,

"Have you noticed how the land gets flatter, the temperature gets lower, and the air becomes less humid the farther we get from the Amazon?"

"You have lived here all your life, while I am only a visitor, so you recognize these changes faster, but now that you mention it, I feel it."

"But I'm seeing a new grass. What about you?"

"We grow it in China and call it rice, which we turn into food by harvesting the grains."

"I'll bring it back for my gatherer-planters."

"China has a better name. We call them farmers when harvesting from a larger field. We'll ask the tribes what they grow..."

They hiked for another week before coming upon a village larger than any found north of the Amazon. A group of villagers came out, and their leader stepped forward as Tiana and Yarima approached. When they stopped, Yarima spoke first.

"My name is Yarima. I come from a village on the banks of the Amazon rainforest." She paused for a moment while pointing.

"With me is Tianshu. He is an explorer from a land called China across the Pacific Ocean, far to the west. Have you heard of it?"

"No, only the Atlantic, which is the ocean the Spanish explorers who attacked us had to cross. Why are you here?"

"To learn about your people and how you live, and to provide help if you need it. Have you ever heard of the European conquistadors?

They are explorers led by Pedro Álvares Cabral, who comes from Portugal."

"No, the explorers who attacked are by Juan Diaz de Solis. Why do you ask?"

"The conquistadors kill villagers north of the river with powerful weapons and infect them with diseases. They plan to take over the villages by killing all the villagers and moving their people in. Does de Solis treat you better?"

"He does the same, but even though his weapons are better, we outnumber his troops and have driven him away."

Tianshu spoke to Yarima before she replied, once again pointing at him.

"His healers have medicine that might help. When he comes back, he will give it for the rice you grow. By the way, he calls your planter-gathers farmers, because you grow crops on large parcels of land."

"I will remember that. We also grow fruit. I'll have one of my people bring some to show you."

One of the village women gave several pieces to Yarima. Tianshu spoke to her before she replied.

"He calls them oranges. Could I take some oranges and rice when we leave? I would like my farmers to grow them."

"Of course. Why don't you eat and rest here before moving on?"

While eating, Yarima and Tianshu sat with the leader. She asked questions whose answers she would give to Tianshu later.

"We plan to continue exploring further south. How far does your tribal network go?"

"You have to hike many days to reach the end, and if you do, those tribes will say you can go even further, finding large villages doing much the same on similar land…"

When she told this to Tianshu, he said,

"We should turn back now. Tell the leader we thank him, and that I will return someday with medicine, even though I don't know when. And tell him we Chinese are much better than the Europeans. We want to help, not colonize."

The expedition headed north early the next day, and when they reached a place to stop for the night, Yarima spoke to Tianshu.
"What will we do when we get back to the river?"
"I am still thinking. I will tell you when I have the plan…"

Chapter 10

"Going Further North"

Tianshu hadn't completed his plan by the time they reached his encampment, so he told Yarima to take the plants and seeds back to her village and then return immediately. When she did, Tianshu brought everyone together.

"I have now completed the plan. South America is too vast to continue exploring from one starting point like we've been doing, so we'll sail on one ship to the northern edge of the continent, anchor at a good location, and explore on foot from there. So, help load the ship. We shall sail on the next high tide."

While everyone hurried away, Yarima and Tianshu stayed put to talk. Yarima's eyes narrowed as she stuttered.

"Wha-What are high tides?"

"Over many, many years, we Chinese have learned about tides from sailing across the Indian Ocean to build trade routes to Africa. Tides are the periodic rise and fall of sea levels. I don't notice them when out at sea, but I do when anchored. There are two high tides and two low tides each day. Rivers like the Amazon also have tides, which you would notice when the current changes direction. You've paddled on the Amazon your entire life. Haven't you observed this?"

"I have, but never thought about it. What causes them?"

"No one knows, but we keep track of when they occur."

Yarima changed her line of questioning to build on what Tianshu had just said.

"My people tell time according to the Sun. We know three—sunrise, sun overhead, and sunset. How do you keep track?"

"With an hourglass, but it's only an estimate. You ask good questions, but let's help prepare for sailing away. Ask me more when we're at sea…"

Yarima did that on the first night, while she and Tianshu were standing on deck, gazing at the heavens above.

"I've never seen such a magnificent display of the stars. We can't see land, so how do you keep the boat headed in the right direction?"

"China has people called astronomers who use tools and star clusters. I have learned enough over the years to navigate."

Yarima sighed before saying,

"Looking at the stars fills me with wonder about the world. How did it begin? How did we get here? Why are we here? You Chinese are smarter than my tribe. Do you have answers?"

"Many Chinese find answers in religion, but we also have people called philosophers, who have spent years coming up with a way of thinking called philosophy that gives some answers. Now is not the time, but someday you might want to study these subjects. Now, let's sleep so we're ready for whatever awaits us tomorrow…"

Each day passed like the previous. After sailing for six days, they reached the top of South America and then sailed west until dropping anchor in a promising river. The guards that would stay behind rowed the expedition to shore, and the tracker started leading them inland.

He came upon a trail that pointed west, and a day later, they reached a small village whose people came out to meet them. Their leader spoke when Tianshu and Yarima approached.

"We are happy to see you. You look different than the conquistadors. Their leader is a man named Pedro Álvares Cabral. They came only once on the trail you took to get here. We don't like them. They started taking things without asking, and Pedro said they would come back to help. When they left, several of my people caught a disease they must have left behind. Will you help us keep them away?"

Yarima interpreted, then answered while pointing.

"I am Yarima from the Amazon rainforest, and this is Tianshu, an explorer from a country called China. We don't like the conquistadors either. They are here to kill and take over your village. We are here to learn about your people and land, and to offer help if you need it. On this visit, we didn't bring the weapons needed to fight, but we will come back to do that after we learn more."

"Why don't you stay and eat with us? Then I will show you some of what we have that you might like."

Yarima and Tianshu sat with the leader, who served them a special food and drink.

"We make this from the beans of a shrub. Have you tasted this before?"

After sampling and sipping, Yarima looked at Tianshu, whose sideways nod said no. Then she said,

"We haven't, but I like the tasty flavor. "How do you make it?"

"We pick the beans from a shrub and then grind them into a powder."

Yarima blurted,

"Would you give me some of the plants? I want to take them back to my village, so my farmers can grow them."

"I'll have one of my people get them for you right now."

They continued eating in silence until a villager returned. Then the leader said,

"Now, I'll show you a powerful substance we make from the beans of another plant. After grinding them, we either sniff or smoke the powder."

One of his men returned with enough for Yarima to sniff cautiously and Tianshu to puff from a pipe.

Yarima's head began spinning after only two sniffs that made her enter a pleasant trance-like state that stopped her talking, but Tianshu kept puffing away, finally saying,

"We Chinese smoke something like this. We call it opium."

Shaking her head enough times to clear her thinking, Yarima said,

"Could I have some of these plants, too?"

The leader gestured, and the man who had brought the powder returned with several.

Yarima then spoke for Tianshu.

"Thank you for your hospitality. We will now head back and look for the conquistadors to figure out what weapons we should bring back to fight them. It might take a year, but I promise to return..."

Returning to the ship, Yarima stored the plants, and the expedition rested until starting to hunt for the conquistadors the next day. Tianshu told his tracker to go far enough ahead so he could run back if he spotted trouble. Near sunset on the second day, he rushed to Tianshu.

"The conquistadors are coming this way. Many are riding gigantic beasts."

Tianshu yelled,

"We must run the other way to our ship. When we get there, I will send our fastest runner to tell the village leader the conquistadors are coming. His people must hide so the conquistadors don't kill them. Then, when our runner returns, we will sail away."

The expedition sailed away a day later. When safely at sea, Tianshu spoke to the entire group.

"We will sail back to our Amazon River encampment for Yarima and her warriors to return to their village. Meanwhile, I must sail back to China to tell my emperor what we have learned, and then to return with more ships loaded with more supplies and weapons. I will also bring the beasts the conquistadors are riding. They are called horses. Are there questions?"

Yarima spoke for all the warriors.

"We have never seen horses. When you return, will you tell us about them and teach us how to ride?"

"He nodded yes and then said,

"Go about your normal life until I return, and when I do, I will send a runner to tell you to join us for battle. I will try to come back within a year, but only the gods or fate knows for sure..."

Chapter 11

"Homecoming Joy"

Waving and cheering, everyone rushed to see Yarima when she and her warriors returned. Yarima returned the joyful greeting by smiling while pointing, but kept her thoughts to herself.

I love my rainforest and my tribe, but leaders must always appear dignified and in control of their emotions and actions, even when not.

The commotion stopped when the priestess stepped forward to lead a chant and spoke when it ended.

"We are glad that you and your warriors have returned. Tell us about your journey."

"We met many tribes and found new plants that give powerful medicine and flavorful food. I will give them to our gatherers so they can grow and harvest. When I sampled the medicine by sniffing, it put me in a trance that gave me strange but pleasant thoughts."

Yarima paused for the priestess to speak.

"I will use it in our rituals to make them even more memorable."

Yarima nodded yes, but then changed the subject.

"All the tribes are glad to see us, and want our help fighting the conquistadors, but they have returned riding gigantic beasts we have never seen. Tianshu calls them horses and tells me they trample everything in their way. When he returns in one year, I must join him to defeat them. And until then, I will stay here and resume my tribal duties..."

When the villagers dispersed after her final words, Yarima retrieved Mandei from her surrogate mother before going to the hut she called home. After rearranging, she started playing with Mandie, whose face and hands showed pure joy. Yarma cried while hugging her child.

I have missed bonding with Mandei. She can now speak in partial words. Until Tianshu returns, I will teach her the ways of the tribe. I hope it is longer than a year…

Tianshu's sailors made every effort to speed the voyage home. The wind and waves cooperated, allowing Tianshu to reach Beijing even sooner than anticipated.

The people who greeted Tianshu were pleased to see him, but expressed it by merely bowing. When the emperor heard of his return, he summoned him the next day to speak at a gathering of his wisest bureaucrats. Knowing this would happen, Tianshu had rehearsed on the voyage back. When the emperor told him to tell about what he had accomplished, Tianshu began speaking in a clear and measured, dignified manner.

"I have learned that South America is a vast continent, with unique landscapes populated by tribes living in villages, not towns or cities. Although they know less and are less sophisticated than our society, they seem smart. They know how to dig silver out of mountains and mines, and they know how to grow rice, which we can always use more of."

Tinashu paused for comments, but other than knowing nods, none came, so he continued.

"They also have plants we do not have. One of them produces a bean that is ground into a powder for making sweet-tasting food and drink. Another plant has leaves that tribes use to make a substance they sniff or smoke, giving the same effects as opium."

Tianshu now paused for a bureaucrat to comment.

"More silver will increase trade, and the substance they smoke and sniff will decrease the cost of opium."

After nodding yes, Tianshu continued.

"But South America has a growing problem. Spanish explorers, led by Juan Diaz de Solis are trying to colonize the country. Some of the tribes I met can fight them off, but Portugal explorers called conquistadors, led by Pedro Álvares Cabral, are trying to do the same, using muskets, swords, and horses to kill the people. The tribes I met don't have these weapons. Do you think I should return to help defeat them?"

Tianshu paused to let the bureaucrats discuss the problem. The emperor listened for only a few minutes before interrupting.

"It will be better for South America and China to stop Europe from colonizing the country. Our weapons are as good as theirs, and we are better horsemen, so I commission you to return with a larger fleet, carrying more weapons and horses to defeat the conquistadors. Bring trainers who can teach horsemanship and battle tactics. Leave immediately."

Tianshu bowed, then said,

"I shall do so as soon as I load the ships. The next time I return to Beijing, I shall bring a glorious victory…"

Chapter 12

"Tianshu's Return"

When Tianshu's messenger reached Yarima, she hid her feelings by gathering the warriors that she had chosen for his previous expedition and prepared as fast as possible to follow him back to Tianshu's encampment. By the time she arrived, excitement about the new expedition had replaced her anger about his returning in less than a year.

Tianshu let them rest briefly before gathering everyone and speaking.

"Welcome, Yarima and her warriors. As promised, I have come back with more ships loaded with supplies and weapons we will give to the tribes, so they can fight the conquistadors. I have also brought horses that we will ride when battling the conquistadors. But before we can, I must teach you to ride the horses and use even better battle tactics than last time, because now we will fight using both horses and ground fighters."

Scanning the gathering, from left to right and front to back, he saw only eager eyes, so he continued.

"To do that, I have brought with me trainers for both horsemanship and battle tactics. We will begin the training tomorrow and stay here until the trainers say you are ready to practice the skills you have just learned.

"Then, we will sail just far enough south to find a flat, grassy field that is the same as where we will fight, and then practice the actual riding and battle tactics you will use. We will practice until the trainers say you are ready to win. And why will we win? Because Chinese horsemanship and our warriors' ferocious fighting ability are already superior to our opponent, and the training shall make you even better. So, sleep well and awaken ready to learn…"

Yarima concentrated harder than ever before for the next five days. Tianshu noticed, but kept his thoughts to himself.

Yarima is an innately smart leader. She is totally engaged in learning. The combination of natural ability and dedicated study will make her unbeatable.

After two additional days, Tianshu gathered everyone once more and spoke.

"The trainers say you are ready to begin practicing what they have been teaching, so tomorrow we sail to a practice field. Rest easy tonight. We shall depart at first light."

The scouting party Tianshu sent several days ago had returned after locating the practice field and marking an onshore location close to where the crews could anchor.

The two vessels dropped anchor early in the afternoon of the second day. A steady onshore wind rippled the bright blue water, making waves that sparkled in the warm sunlight streaming from a cloudless sky. Then, the horsemanship trainers on each vessel began giving instructions to the warriors. Yarima absorbed every word when hers began speaking.

"I have picked the warriors who will ride horses in battle. You know who you are, so now I want you to choose a horse you will like. It is the only one you will ride. You and the horse must get to know each other and build a bond of trust that makes you as one. Take a bridle from the pile and use it to help your horse swim to shore while everyone else takes supplies and sets up our tent camp."

Grabbing a bridle, Yarima led those chosen to the horses and noticed how they were behaving.

The horses are whinnying while shaking their heads and pawing the air with their hooves, but I'm not scared…

—

After picking her horse, she rubbed its head while talking like she did to her daughter. Her mount settled down enough for her to put on the bridle. Then, when the other warriors had bridled up, she led them to the plank they would use to slip into the water and then swim ashore.

All the warriors had swum for years, so getting the horses to shore was the easiest part of getting to camp. Once there, Yarima picked a tent and kept patting her horse. By the time all supplies had been carried, Yarima and her horse were like one.

When the trainers saw that the riders were ready, one of them gave more instructions.

"Tie the bridle to the stake near your tent and let your horse graze. Tomorrow, we will show you how to put on a saddle. For the first couple of days, you will ride naked while practicing with the ground fighters. Now, we will have dinner, and after that, keep bonding with your horse until dark..."

Yarima slept next to her horse while thinking about the day's excitement.

Horses are a pleasure to care for...we could use them in the rainforest...can they sleep standing up?...I'll ask a trainer tomorrow.

When she found one the next morning, she asked her question.

"Horses sleep standing up, but sometimes they sleep lying down. They're not as smart as dogs, but over time they'll get to know what you're saying."

His answer prompted another.

"What are dogs?"

"They are animals we Chinese have had for years. We use them for hunting and guarding."

"Do you think they'd like my tribe?"

"Dogs seem to like all people. Maybe Tianshu will bring some back on his next expedition..."

For the next five days, Yarima stopped asking questions and focused only on battle practice, thinking while doing so.

Battle practice is thrilling...I hope I'll feel the same when the battle starts...

Tianshu observed the practice from a distance close enough to watch her.

She rides like the best Chinese horsemen. Her physical ability makes her a natural…and she uses swords, lances, and spears like she's done it for years…

At the end of the fifth day, the trainer said,

"Starting tomorrow, you will practice while wearing what the conquistadors wear. Our Chinese horsemen dress differently. After a couple of days, you will decide if you want to swap some of the conquistador gear for what we Chinese wear…"

Yarima wore boots, pants, and an armored chest plate as well as metal arm protectors over a long-sleeve shirt. She also wore a helmet that felt awkward and heavy, but after several hours, all the gear felt comfortable.

Yarima's mastery of fighting on horseback kept improving. No one could match her swift sword strokes or lance jabs. The trainers watched all the warriors, and after two more days, made the decision.

"You have practiced enough. Each of you can decide what to wear in battle."

Tianshu spoke next.

"We sail tomorrow on the first tide that is in our favor. Our destination—the village where we sampled tasty food, and I smoked something like opium. The trail we took there led us to the conquistadors, who were riding horses. What we do when we get to the village will depend upon what we find. I hope some villagers survived if the conquistadors had come back. If so, we will train some to join the battle…

Chapter 13

"The Last Battle"

Yarima did nothing but talk to her warriors and horse while sailing to their destination. When Tianshu noticed her total focus on the upcoming battle, he didn't interrupt.

But as soon as they arrived, Yarima found Tianshu and said,

"You should have a tracker lead you and me and a few of my armed warriors to the village so we can talk to the leader."

Tianshu nodded before saying,

"We think alike. That's what I was planning to do. We will leave tomorrow at dawn…"

The tracker remembered the way, so they reached the village not long before sunset on the first day. Yarima saw that most of the huts had been destroyed, but hearing them approach, the leader and several men came to meet them. Yarima didn't wait for Tianshu to tell her what to say. She pointed at Tianshu as she began to speak.

"I am Yarima, and with me is Tianshu. Do you remember our first visit?"

The leader stepped closer before saying,

"Welcome. You promised to come back, and now you have."

Yarima smiled when she replied.

"We sailed here in boats loaded with more supplies, better weapons, and also horses. We are now ready to battle the conquistadors.

Horses are the gigantic beasts the conquistadors ride to trample everything in their way. Did they destroy your village?"

"They came a few days ago on the trail you took to reach us. Did you see them?"

"No, they must be further to the east. How many of your men can join us to fight?"

"As many as you want, including me. I am a fighter as well as the leader."

"I will ask Tianshu."

A moment later, he flashed both hands three times. Understanding this universal counting sign, he talked to his men, who hurried back to the village. When he walked back to Yarima, she spoke immediately.

"We will train your fighters as soon as we take them to our ships. We will leave as soon as your fighters get here. Make sure you bring your fastest tracker and messenger."

The leader left to pick a tracker and messenger, giving Yarima time to explain to Tianshu. He spoke as soon as she finished.

"We can train them in a day, and once we include them in our battle tactics, we will unload the boats and take the trail further east."

Yarima's nod signaled she agreed, but she kept her thoughts to herself.

I have something better than that, but I won't say until later.

Though darkness had fallen, the leader's tracker led the procession, and they arrived with the rising sun. Tianshu assembled the entire expedition to explain what would happen next.

"After we eat, our trainers will teach fighting skills using the new weapons to the men who have just come. Then our battle tacticians will place them into fighting groups built around Yarima's warriors on horseback. After that, we will bring the weapons and horses ashore and have your tracker lead us to the conquistadors."

Yarima interrupted before he could say more. She spoke slowly while mustering all her leadership skills.

"No. We must have the new tracker and messenger race away right now to locate them. Fighter training also begins right now. When they locate the conquistadors, they will mark a place on the shore where we can unload. After they do, they must rush back to tell us. Then, we sail to the spot, unload the weapons and horses, and prepare for battle. And then, we attack…"

Yarima spoke only to herself as she observed the fight training; she also watched the weather.

The weather's changing…the wind is getting stronger, blowing in clouds…might this signal a storm is approaching? No matter what it becomes, we must fight as soon as we are ready. I hope the excitement I'm feeling and the thrill of battle will keep fear from striking…

The messenger arrived at dusk, signaling to his leader that they had located the conquistadors. Tianshu, who had stayed close to the leader, saw it too, and he immediately yelled to alert everyone. When they clustered around him, Tianshu spoke.

"The messenger just arrived. He and the tracker have found our enemy. We sail to the place they have marked as soon as the tracker gets back…"

Unloading the horses and preparing for battle began at the start of the next day's dark and cloudy dawn. Tianshu watched as Yarima and the battle tactics trainer took charge of preparation, which took only minutes. From the lead position in the procession of battle groups, Yarima pointed at the tracker and then to the path that would take them to the conquistadors. Then she kicked her heels into her horse. The tracker ran as fast as he could to lead the way.

Yarima stopped just far enough from Pedro's guards to avoid detection while studying the camp. Her pointing told the other warriors to space themselves parallel to the camp. After doing so, Yarima drew her sword and led the charge.

The attack stunned Pedro and his conquistadors. The guard's screams came too late for them to mount up in time. Yarima's warriors swept in, trampling those running to their horses as well as the ground fighters loading their muskets.

Pedro thought he was too valuable to be merely a fighter, so he stayed far enough back to avoid being attacked, but close enough to see the action. His expression shifted from stunned surprise to shocked anger. His jaw dropped as he gasped.

—

Where did the attackers come from? Isn't that Yarima leading the charge? Where did she get the weapons and horses? She's already knocked two of my men off their mounts…I must stop this, but how? Ah-ha, I know.

Fully engaged, Yarima swept further forward, slashing with her sword while also observing the action. She had dodged all jabs or bullets from opponents, either riding horses or firing muskets. Suddenly, she spotted someone close by about to fire at her. It was too late to wheel her horse away, so she took the only action possible— she leaped off.

Pedro's bullet missed Yarima, but it struck her horse, bringing it to a dead stop in its tracks. It reared on its hind legs before collapsing sideways, trapping Yarima underneath. When Pedro saw the horse had pinned Yarima, he grabbed a sword from a dead conquistador and ran toward her.

Yarima was struggling to free herself, but couldn't. She was still trying when, seemingly out of nowhere, someone knelt beside her. She had barely enough strength to turn her head to see, and when she did, her eyes widened as she stuttered one word.

"Pu-Pedro—" he covered her mouth with one hand and then said,

"Know this before you die, I will cut your heart out and—" Pedro's words stuck in his throat. Tianshu had just booted him away from Yarima. But it was not enough to stop Pedro. Grabbing his sword, he staggered to his feet and glared at Tianshu.

"You must be the one who gave horses to Yarima. Well, I will make sure this never happens again."

He moved cautiously toward Tianshu, unaware that Yarima's sword was at Tianshu's feet. Tianshu grabbed it and stood facing Pedro before taking a swordman's fighting stance. Then, after a salute to his opponent, Tianshu spoke.

"You have brought your best, I trust? Please, let us begin."

THE END